The Sapphire Princess Meets a Monster

THE JEWEL KINGDOM

The Sapphire Princess Meets a Monster

JAHNNA N. MALCOLM

Illustrations by Neal McPheeters

ISBN 0-590-21284-2

Text copyright © 1997 by Jahnna Beecham and Malcolm Hillgartner.
All rights reserved. Published by Scholastic Inc.
LITTLE APPLE PAPERBACKS is a trademark of Scholastic Inc.

12 11 10 9 8 7 6 5 4 3   9/9 0 1 2/0

Printed in the U.S.A.   40
First Scholastic printing, June 1997

For
Karen Kay Cody
and
Princess Gemma

CONTENTS

The Sapphire Princess Meets a Monster

THE JEWEL KINGDOM

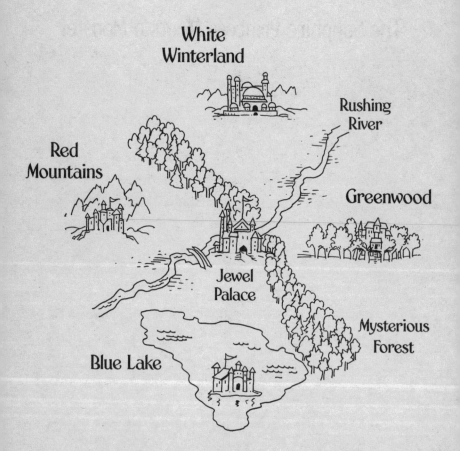

White Winterland

Rushing River

Red Mountains

Greenwood

Jewel Palace

Mysterious Forest

Blue Lake

The Golden Gift

"It's a perfect day for a picnic!" Princess Sabrina said as she sailed across Blue Lake. She was riding in her laurel-leaf boat.

Gurt the Gilliwag sat behind her, paddling the boat. The green froglike creature was a close friend of the Sapphire Princess.

"My dear lady," Gurt said in his deep

voice, "this very golden afternoon matches your golden gift."

That morning a golden basket had mysteriously arrived at the gates of the Sapphire Palace. A card was pinned to the basket. It read, *To the Sapphire Princess. Signed, A Secret Admirer.*

The golden basket was filled with bread, cheese, and chocolate. Each piece was wrapped in gold cloth and tied with a sapphire-blue ribbon.

Princess Sabrina loved the basket. She invited her three sisters to join her for a picnic that afternoon.

Demetra, the Diamond Princess and Emily, the Emerald Princess, had arrived. While they waited for the Ruby Princess, the three sisters sailed across the lake to Bluebonnet Falls.

"Let's have a race!" Sabrina called to

the Emerald Princess. Emily was on her knees, paddling a large green lily pad.

"I'm ready when you are," Princess Emily said as she pulled up next to Sabrina. "Just say the word."

Of the four Jewel Princesses, Emily was the most athletic. She ruled the Greenwood and spent her days climbing trees and riding horses through her lush green forest.

The Diamond Princess steered her boat made of white gardenias between her two sisters. Demetra ruled the White Winterland and everything she wore was glittering white.

"I think we should wait for Roxanne," Demetra advised. "Wasn't she going to join us?"

"Roxanne is *always* late," Emily said

with a frown. "If we wait for her, it will be sundown before we get to eat."

Sabrina focused her pale blue eyes on the shore. There was no sign of her sister Roxanne.

"I agree with Emily," Sabrina announced, tossing her long blond hair over her shoulders. "Let's have a race ourselves."

"No, no, no!" A yellow and pink butterfly squeaked as she landed on Sabrina's finger. It was Zazz, Princess Sabrina's palace advisor and best friend.

"Princess, if you race in this boat, you'll lose," Zazz sputtered. "Or sink. Just look what we're carrying. Gurt. That heavy gold basket. The napkins and tablecloths, and all of the royal china."

Sabrina put her face nose-to-nose with

the tiny butterfly. "Then I'll just have to get another boat. Any idea where I might find one?"

Blue Lake was dotted with boats. "I'll call the Nymphs," Zazz said as she fluttered off the princess's finger. "They'll bring a leaf boat right over."

"Don't do that," Emily called. "Sabrina, hop on my lily pad. We'll race Demetra together."

Sabrina stood up to leap onto Emily's boat, but something tugged at her arm.

Sabrina spun around. No one was there. Just Gurt the Gilliwag calmly paddling away. She looked at the mysterious golden basket. It glittered in the afternoon sun.

"Come on, Sabrina!" Emily cried. "Jump!"

Before Sabrina could make a move, the basket danced across the bottom of the boat and leaped into her hands.

"Did you see that?" Emily gasped to Demetra.

"I don't like this one bit," Demetra said, shaking her thick brown braid. "Sabrina, you should leave that basket alone. You don't know where it came from."

"Don't be such a worrywart!" Sabrina stared at the golden basket. "This is a present. A very magical present from a secret admirer. Full of wonderful food."

"And I'm starving," Zazz called from her perch on the boat's bow.

"Me, too." Sabrina leaned forward and whispered to the butterfly, "Zazz, let's not wait until we get to Bluebonnet Falls. Why don't you and I take a piece of chocolate from the picnic basket right now?"

Zazz rubbed her little legs together. "I like chocolate. Yes, yes!"

Sabrina opened the basket. But just as her fingers touched the food, something jolted the boat.

"Whoa!" Zazz fell backward onto the floor of the boat and bent one antenna. "What was that?"

"I'm not sure!" Sabrina replied.

Thunk!

Something hit the boat again.

"I'm afraid something is trying to sink us," Gurt declared, pulling his paddle into the boat.

"The Water Sprites must be playing a joke." Sabrina peered into the water. She was looking for the ghostly outline of the little Sprites.

"If the Sprites don't want you to see them, Princess, you won't," Zazz said as she tried to straighten her antenna.

"I'll try calling them." Sabrina cupped her hands around her mouth. "Hello? Anybody there?"

Nothing.

The Sapphire Princess leaned over the side of the boat. She was so close, her nose nearly touched the lake.

All at once two huge yellow eyes appeared just below the surface.

Sabrina screamed and fell backward in a faint.

The Blue Lake Monster

"Sabrina, wake up!" Demetra fanned Sabrina's face with a broad green leaf.

Zazz fluttered nervously over their heads.

"Is the princess all right?" the butterfly asked.

Gurt pointed toward the Sapphire Palace. "Should I swim for help?"

"No, wait!" Princess Emily scooped a

handful of ice-cold water from the lake. She tossed the water onto Sabrina's face. "Sabrina, open your eyes!"

Her eyelids fluttered open. "A face," Sabrina gasped. "I saw a face as big as this boat. It was under the water."

"I'll see what it was!" Gurt cried. The Gilliwag dove over the side and instantly disappeared from sight.

Demetra poured Sabrina a cup of honey nectar. "What did the face look like?"

Sabrina took the cup and slowly sat up. "Well, it was huge and gray. And very lumpy."

"Did it have a mouth?" Emily asked.

Sabrina nodded. "Yes. And its teeth looked razor sharp."

"What about its body?" Zazz asked, perching on Sabrina's shoulder. "Did you see it?"

Sabrina sipped the nectar. "I didn't see its body, but if its head was as big as this boat, then the body would have to be as big as ten boats."

Zazz frowned. "There's nothing that big that lives in the lake except . . ." Her eyes widened. "The Blue Lake Monster!"

They heard a splash behind them and everyone jumped. The Gilliwag draped his long green arms over the side.

"I saw a shadow," Gurt gasped. "I tried to follow, but it disappeared into the Deep Dark."

The Deep Dark was an inky stretch of water where none of the lake folk ever swam. It was very deep, black as night, and very, very cold.

Now Zazz's eyes were as huge as lily pads. "Then it *was* the Blue Lake Monster!"

Sabrina tapped Zazz on the top of the head with her fingertip. "What's all this talk about a Blue Lake Monster? I've never heard of it."

Zazz shivered. "It's terrible. Just terrible."

"The monster has always been down there," Gurt explained. "Some say it is an evil demon left over from when Lord Bleak ruled the land."

"Lord Bleak!" Demetra gasped. "How awful!"

Lord Bleak and his Darklings had been banished from the Jewel Kingdom years before. That was when Queen Jemma and King Regal had come to the throne. They had divided up the Jewel Kingdom, giving each of their daughters her own jewel and her own land.

"If it has anything to do with Lord Bleak it must be mean and horrible," Emily said, clutching her sisters' hands.

Gurt shrugged. "I don't know. I've never heard of the monster harming anyone."

"Then maybe it's a friendly monster," Sabrina said.

Zazz put her face close to Sabrina's. "But you said that it was gray and had fierce teeth. Something that ugly has to be bad."

"I think you should warn your people," Demetra advised.

Sabrina didn't like to jump to conclusions. She preferred to think things over before taking any action. "I just saw a face," she said. "It could have been a Sprite playing a trick, trying to scare us."

Zazz reluctantly agreed. "They have been known to do that."

Sabrina smiled at her sisters and friends. "We're almost to Bluebonnet Falls. We were going on a picnic. So why don't we eat our lunch and talk about it?"

She picked up the picnic basket and set it in her lap.

Suddenly a huge gray head burst out of the water.

"The Blue Lake Monster!" Zazz squealed.

The monster opened its jaws and let loose a terrible roar.

Sabrina dropped the picnic basket and reached for the purse she wore at her waist. Inside was magic dust that the great wizard Gallivant had given her. She tossed the dust over herself and her guests.

"From Water to Air," she chanted.

Sabrina, Emily, Demetra, and Gurt instantly rose into the sky. Zazz fluttered beside them.

Sabrina extended one arm to the heavens. *"Higher and higher, let us go."*

The group flew far above the monster's head. From her place in the sky, Sabrina could see the dark shadow of the monster beneath the water. The creature was bigger than she ever imagined. Its body seemed to stretch halfway across the lake.

"What shall we do, Princess Sabrina?" Zazz cried. "Where shall we go?"

The Sapphire Princess faced her palace, which sat like a bridge over Blue Lake. "Demetra and Emily, fly back to my palace with Gurt. Zazz, come with me."

"But where will you go?" Demetra asked.

Sabrina pointed to the far shore of Blue Lake. "To the Storkz. They'll know what to do!"

Call the Storkz!

The Storkz lived in Misty Marsh. It was always damp and always covered in a pale green cloud.

"Sage is the leader of the Storkz," Sabrina said as they glided into the marsh. "We need to talk to him."

Zazz clung to the sleeve of Sabrina's gown. "I hope we find him soon," the butterfly mumbled. "It's cold and scary here. I can't see two feet in front of me."

"Don't worry, friend," Sabrina cooed. "There's nothing to fear."

Suddenly a creature with long yellow legs and a thin body covered in blue feathers magically appeared out of the mist. Its big round eyes peered at them from behind tiny gold-rimmed glasses.

"*Sage!*" Sabrina gasped.

"Have you been there all along?" Zazz squeaked, hopping to Sabrina's shoulder. "I didn't see you."

"We are all here." Sage gestured with one wing to the clumps of reeds around him.

Suddenly Sabrina could see dozens of Storkz. All standing tall and still.

"We hear through the waters that you are worried about our Lake Creature," Sage said, staring at her solemnly.

"That's no creature," Zazz cut in. "It's a terrible monster."

"Zazz!" Sabrina tapped the butterfly lightly on her head. "Careful what you say. We're not sure it's terrible."

"The princess is right," Sage advised. "Let us not be too hasty. That creature has lived in Blue Lake a very long time."

"Is it older than the Storkz?" Zazz asked, wide-eyed.

Sage nodded. "Much older. It's been here since the beginning."

"That's why it's so big," Zazz whispered in Sabrina's ear. "With all of that time, what else was there to do but grow!"

"This creature has not shown itself to humans in eons." Sage peered over the top of his glasses. "There must be a reason for this."

"Of course there's a reason," Zazz sputtered. "That awful monster has been sent by Lord Bleak to hurt our princess."

Sabrina wanted to say that wasn't true. But she had to admit, the creature *did* frighten her.

"It attacked my boat," Sabrina told Sage. "And then it leaped out of the water and roared at me."

"Hmm. . . . This is not good." Sage murmured. "I must talk to the Storkz."

In an instant, all of the pale blue birds vanished from sight.

"Do you think the Storkz are still here?" Zazz whispered.

"Yes," Sabrina whispered back. "I can't see them, but I feel them all around us."

"Go back to your palace, Princess," Sage said when he returned. "We will try to speak to the Lake Creature."

Sabrina bowed to the leader of the Storkz. "Thank you. I will do as you say."

"What do you mean, you'll do as he says?" Zazz demanded as they flew back to the Blue Palace. "Sage just wants us to sit and wait!"

"We must be sure about this creature before we scare our people," Sabrina explained. "Promise me, Zazz, that you'll keep this secret."

"Too late," the butterfly said as the palace came into view. "It looks like the secret is out."

Sabrina looked down. The shallow water around the palace was crowded with blue-skinned Nymphs and gawky Gilliwags. They waved huge willow wands in the air. Big-footed Striders skated under the drawbridge, clutching oars in their hands. Even the Water Sprites, pale and ghostlike, had joined the mob.

"We must all hunt for this monster!" Gurt shouted from the center of the crowd.

"Find the monster!" the crowd shouted back.

"And when we find this beast," Gurt added, "we must kill it!"

Fear gripped Sabrina as the mob howled, "Kill the beast!"

Monster Hunt

Princess Sabrina and her sisters huddled together by her bedroom window. Below they could see the crowd guarding the palace.

"It's very sweet that my people want to protect me," Sabrina remarked. "But I'm worried."

"I'm worried, too," Princess Demetra said. "That monster could destroy all of those willow wands with one swift bite."

Sabrina leaned her head against the frame of her open window. She thought about what Sage had told her.

"Why would this monster, who has lived peacefully for so many years, suddenly appear?" she asked her sisters.

"Maybe it wants to tell you something," Emily suggested.

Sabrina nodded. "That's what I've been thinking. But what?"

"I think it wants you to go home. Back to the Jewel Palace," Demetra said. "And that's what I would do if I were you."

Sabrina squeezed her sister's hand. "I can't leave, Demetra. This is my land. When I was crowned Sapphire Princess, I promised to protect the Blue Lake and all of the creatures who live here."

"Even *that* creature?" Emily pointed at

the lake. Just below the surface, as big as a ship, was the Blue Lake Monster!

Demetra backed away from the window. "Sabrina, I'm scared! Why has it come to the palace?"

Sabrina watched the shadow glide swiftly toward the drawbridge. "It's after my people," she gasped. "I've got to stop it!"

"But how?" Emily cried. "You're just one little girl. And that thing is monstrous."

"I have to do something." Sabrina climbed onto the window ledge and peered out. "The Gilliwags and the Nymphs don't even see it!"

Emily caught hold of Sabrina's ankle. "Careful, sister, you might fall."

Sabrina's big blue eyes widened.

"That's it," she said. "I'll leap out of my window and distract it."

"But it will gobble you whole," Demetra warned.

"I won't land in the water." Sabrina patted the little purse at her waist. "I'll use my magic dust and fly across the lake."

"Then the monster will follow you," Emily said.

Sabrina smiled. "That's the idea."

"Do you have enough magic dust to make it across the lake?" Demetra asked.

"If I run out," Sabrina replied, "then I guess I'll have to swim."

Demetra covered her face and groaned, "Oh, no."

"I'll lead it near the Willow-that-Weeps," Sabrina said, thinking out loud. "Then maybe it will get caught in the Spinning Pool and disappear forever."

Suddenly the shadow beneath the water froze. It slowly turned. Two big yellow eyes rose to the surface of the lake.

It was looking straight up at Sabrina!

"Sabrina, I don't like your plan," Demetra said in a shaky voice. "Please climb down from that window."

Sabrina's gaze was locked with the monster's. "I can't," she whispered. "It's watching me."

Very slowly Sabrina opened the purse at her waist. She carefully scooped up a handful of magic dust. All the while she whispered instructions to her sisters.

"When I leave, you two go to the courtyard and guard my people," Sabrina murmured, barely moving her lips. "Tell them to stay on land. That's one place we know the monster won't go."

Suddenly the monster raised its head out of the water. Its big, spiky teeth sparkled in the sunlight.

It's going to get me! Sabrina thought, nearly falling back into the room.

"She's fainting," Emily cried.

"No, I'm not." Sabrina squeezed her eyes closed and willed herself to be brave. She clutched the side of the windowsill with one hand and faced the monster.

"Sabrina, be sensible," Demetra pleaded. "You have to save yourself!"

"I will," Sabrina replied, as she flung the magic dust in the air. "But first I have to save my people."

Sparkle of Light

 Sabrina looked down and smiled. Her plan was working. The monster was following her!

She flew closer to the water to make sure the monster could see her. The big, dark shadow mirrored her every move. If she turned, it turned. If she flew faster, it swam faster.

Across the lake Sabrina could see a

patch of churning water by the Willow-that-Weeps. The Spinning Pool! She was about to head for it when something caught her eye.

A sparkle! A very golden sparkle.

Princess Sabrina shielded her eyes with her hand. The golden light was blinding. Where was it coming from?

Flash!

There it was again. Sabrina squinted toward the shore.

"My boat!" she cried. It was caught in the reeds by Bluebonnet Falls. "That golden light is coming from my boat!"

Inside the boat was the golden basket. It was glowing.

Suddenly Sabrina was being pulled out of the sky!

"What's happening to me?" she cried

as the light pulled her closer and closer to shore! "Stop!"

When she was just over the boat, the golden basket leaped into her hands. "My goodness!" she cried, in surprise.

Sabrina gently landed on the grassy shore. For a moment, she forgot all about the Blue Lake Monster. And thought only of the golden basket.

Sabrina knelt and placed the basket in front of her. Carefully she lifted the lid.

"Oh!"

There, tied with a sapphire-blue ribbon, was the most beautiful pear the princess had ever seen. Its skin shimmered like polished gold.

She couldn't take her eyes off it.

Sabrina's mouth began to water. Her fingers twitched.

"I have to eat it," she murmured, picking up the pear.

Sabrina was just about to take a juicy bite when she heard a huge splash in the lake.

"Nooooooo!" the monster roared, shooting out of the water. It towered above Sabrina's head. Then opened its jaws and bent forward.

The princess froze with the pear in midair.

This is it, she thought, staring into the beast's mouth. *It's going to gobble me up.*

She squeezed her eyes shut and waited.

But she only felt a slight tug. At her fingers.

Sabrina opened her eyes and stared at her empty hand.

"My pear!" she gasped.

The Lake Monster had eaten it. The beast had swallowed the golden fruit in one gulp. And now something odd was happening to the monster.

Its gray skin turned green. Then it changed to a sickly yellow.

The monster swayed back and forth, its eyes rolling back in its head. Slowly, slowly, it fell forward.

"Ooomph!"

First the body hit the ground. Then the long neck stretched across the grass.

Finally the monster's head came to rest, with its nose in Princess Sabrina's lap.

6

The Poisoned Pear

Sabrina stared at the Lake Monster's head. It was as big as a boat. It lay with its eyes closed, breathing in shaky gusts of air through its nose.

Sabrina carefully reached up and touched the monster's nose. The yellow skin was soft, like the petals of a flower.

The monster sighed at her touch.

"Poor monster," Sabrina whispered. "You're sick."

The ragged breathing grew calmer.

Sabrina's heart went out to this creature. It looked so sad and helpless.

"There's the princess!" a voice cried, from behind her. "The monster has her in his clutches."

Sabrina turned to see her sisters rounding the bend by Bluebonnet Falls. They were leading many creatures from Blue Lake.

"Don't worry, Sabrina, we'll save you!" Emily shouted as she hiked up her skirt and raced to help the Sapphire Princess.

Zazz the Butterfly clung to the top of Emily's wild red hair and ordered, "Faster! Run faster!"

Gurt and several other Gilliwags

hopped behind Emily and Zazz, waving wooden oars in the air.

"Save the princess!" Gurt bellowed. "Kill the monster!"

"Stay back!" Sabrina cried, wrapping her arms around the monster's head. She pressed her cheek against its skin. She could hardly hear it breathe. "This creature is ill. Please, don't hurt it."

Princess Emily and the crowd stumbled to a stop. They were confused.

"But . . . but I don't understand," Emily stammered. "I thought that monster was trying to hurt you."

Sabrina looked at her sister with sad eyes. "That's what I thought, too. But I think it was only trying to help me."

Zazz fluttered above the golden basket that had fallen over on its side. The pears had tumbled onto the ground. Dead flies and ants lay around the golden fruit.

"Look, everyone!" Zazz cried. "This food . . . it was poisoned."

Demetra narrowed her eyes at the golden basket. "I knew something was wrong. That gift wasn't from a secret admirer."

"It was from a secret enemy," Emily finished.

"And it was *sooo* beautiful," Zazz murmured.

Sabrina stroked the monster's lumpy head. "You knew that pear was poisoned, didn't you? You ate it to save me."

Sabrina thought back to the first time the monster had bumped her boat. It was when she touched the golden basket. Then the monster reared out of the water when Sabrina and Zazz were about to sneak a bite of chocolate.

"We were all wrong," Sabrina announced to her people. "This creature never tried to hurt me. Everything it did was to help me."

The monster moaned and rolled its head to one side.

Sabrina knew it was in great pain. Tears welled up in her eyes.

"You poor, dear creature," she said. "I wish there were something I could do to help you."

"Perhaps there is," a voice whispered across the wind.

Sabrina lifted her head and looked toward the lake. There, half-hidden in the reeds, was Sage.

"At the base of Bluebonnet Falls grows a tiny purple flower," the wisest of the Storkz said. "It has the power to heal." The monster groaned again and he added,

"But you must be quick. There isn't much time."

Sabrina could have asked Gurt, or even Zazz, to go to the Falls. But this was one thing she had to do herself.

The monster had saved her life. Now she would return the favor.

7

The Spirit of Blue Lake

 The purple flower grew only in one spot, directly behind the waterfall. To pick it, Sabrina had to dive through the rushing water.

Now the princess knelt before the dying monster. Her chiffon dress was soaked and clung to her body. Her blond hair hung dripping down her back. But she didn't care. Sabrina had the magic flower.

It took all her strength to pry open the monster's thick jaws. Finally she was able to place the flower on its tongue.

"Swallow this," she urged. "It will make you well."

Demetra and Emily stood with Zazz and the other Lake Dwellers at a safe distance. Even though the monster was ill, they still didn't trust it.

Sabrina stroked the monster's brow. "Please, try to swallow. I want you to live. You *have* to live."

After a few seconds, the creature swallowed.

"Good. You did it!" Sabrina cheered. "Now relax and let the flower work its magic."

Sabrina and her friends watched and waited. The cure seemed to take forever. But ever so slowly, the sickly yellow skin

turned back into a nice dark gray.

Sabrina kept petting the monster's head. Its breathing was becoming less harsh.

"That's a good monster," she cooed. "You're getting better. I can see it."

A low growl rattled the monster's throat. And all of the Lake Dwellers leaped back in alarm.

"Sabrina, be careful!" Demetra warned.

Sabrina ignored her sister and kept stroking the monster's nose and brow.

With each breath, it seemed to grow stronger. Soon its body began to twitch. Then its eyelids fluttered.

"It's waking up," Sabrina announced.

Demetra, Emily, and the others took another giant step backward.

Sabrina held her breath.

At last the monster opened its eyes. It looked at Sabrina and big tears welled up in its yellow eyes.

"Please, don't look at me, Princess," the creature said in a high, lilting voice.

Sabrina blinked in surprise. The Lake Monster was a girl!

"I am too ugly," the monster continued.

"But . . . but you're not ugly!" Sabrina cried. "You're beautiful."

The monster sighed. A deep sigh, full of sorrow. "There was a time when you might have said I was beautiful and everyone would have agreed with you." Her huge eyes narrowed. "That was before Lord Bleak and the Darklings ruled this land."

"You mean you haven't always looked like this?" Sabrina asked.

"Oh, no," the monster replied in her lovely voice. "I was once a mermaid with sea-green eyes and skin the color of pearls. I was called Oona."

"Oona!" Zazz blurted. "I've heard stories of Oona."

Gurt nodded. "Oona is the Spirit of Blue Lake. They say she has been here since the beginning of time."

Oona nodded. "That I have. That I have."

"But why have we never seen or heard from you?" Sabrina asked.

Oona hung her head. "Because I am a monster. After Lord Bleak cast his spell on me, I tried to talk to my friends. But I scared them. They all ran from me."

"But we wouldn't run . . ." Sabrina didn't finish her sentence. She realized that she *had* run from Oona. And so had her people. They all had been ready to destroy Oona just because of the way she looked.

"We made a mistake," Sabrina declared, looking at the crowd. "We thought just because the golden picnic basket was beautiful, it was good."

Zazz hung her head. "We were wrong."

Sabrina looked back at Oona. "And we thought just because you looked different from us, you were bad."

"And we were wrong again," Gurt added.

Sabrina knelt in front of the huge creature. Demetra, Emily, and all the creatures of Blue Lake knelt, too.

"Dear Oona, will you accept our sincerest apology?" Sabrina asked.

The corners of Oona's gray lips curled into a smile. "Of course, my princess. And let me say that after years of hiding in the Deep Dark, at last I can say I am happy."

Everyone cheered. Sabrina stood up and clapped her hands in delight. "Oh, I wish we could celebrate this moment with a feast!"

Gurt stepped forward. "Princess, we still have the china and the tablecloths."

"And all of the guests are here," Zazz added.

"That's true. But we have no food to offer anyone." Sabrina pointed to the picnic basket and the poisoned food beside it. "Not one crumb."

Suddenly a shadow darkened the sky. It swooped over their heads with a rush of wind.

"Look out!" The Lake Dwellers clutched their heads and huddled in fear.

Sabrina looked up, frightened. But her

fear soon turned to joy. She skipped over to her sisters and pointed skyward.

Emily laughed out loud. "Look who's here!"

Demetra opened one eye and peeked at the sky. "Well," she huffed. "It's about time!"

Four Crown Jewels

A great fire-breathing dragon circled above the crowd. Riding on its back, laughing and waving, was Roxanne, the Ruby Princess.

Sabrina raced to greet her sister as soon as the dragon touched down. "You're here at last!"

Roxanne wore a ruby-red traveling dress complete with red gloves and cape.

She tossed the cape over her shoulder and hugged Sabrina. "It's so good to see you! Did I miss anything?"

"Miss anything?" Demetra repeated as she and Emily ran to join their sisters. "We've had an entire adventure while waiting for you."

Roxanne's dark eyes sparkled. "Oh, we love a good adventure." She turned to the green and red dragon. "Don't we, Hapgood?"

Hapgood was Roxanne's friend and palace advisor. He lived with the Ruby Princess in the Red Mountains.

The dragon nodded very formally to the princess. "My lady, life with you is one great adventure. I do enjoy it. It keeps me young."

Roxanne patted the dragon's neck. "That's the spirit, Happy."

Emily draped her arm around Sabrina's shoulder. "Look at us. We're all together."

"Yes." Sabrina smiled fondly at her sisters. "Here we are, the four jewels of our kingdom."

Demetra nodded. "Now we have two reasons to celebrate. It's really too bad about our picnic, though."

"What happened?" Roxanne asked.

The other three looked at each other. Sabrina spoke first. "It's a very long story. Let me just say that our basket of food was poisoned."

"Who would have done such a thing?" Roxanne asked.

Demetra lowered her voice. "Lord Bleak and his Darklings."

"Oh!" Roxanne gasped, putting one gloved hand to her mouth. "Flying here we passed over the Mysterious Forest. Hapgood was certain he saw several Darklings running into the woods."

"They wore black capes, and seemed terribly upset about something," Hapgood added.

"They were upset because their awful trick didn't work," Demetra cut in. "They tried to poison Sabrina!"

"Luckily, Oona was there to save me," Sabrina declared.

"Oona?" Roxanne cocked her head. "Who is Oona?"

Sabrina pointed to the spot where the Lake Creature had been resting. It was empty.

"She was just over there by the shore, but she's gone," Sabrina said. "I hope she hasn't run away."

Emily leaned forward and whispered,

"She's very shy, because of the way she looks."

"What does she look like?" Roxanne whispered back.

The three princesses paused, trying to find the words to describe the lake creature.

Before, Sabrina would have described Oona as gray and lumpy with fierce, pointed teeth. But now when she thought of Oona, she could only remember her eyes.

"She has big, golden eyes," Sabrina said. "They are very warm and friendly. But there is also a touch of sadness in them. Her skin is like rose petals, soft and velvety."

"She's quite large," Demetra added. "Bigger than you, Hapgood. But that doesn't slow her down in the water."

Emily nodded. "She moves very fast and very gracefully through Blue Lake. She is afraid that she's ugly, but we think she's beautiful."

Sabrina was glad to see her sisters had changed their minds about the Blue Lake Monster. Now that they knew Oona, they admired and loved her, too.

Sabrina squinted out over the lake. "It's a shame we don't have any food. I was hoping Oona would join us for dinner."

"If it's food you need," Roxanne said, "I've got just the thing. Happy, show my sisters what we brought."

Hapgood unfolded one large red wing. Underneath were two huge picnic baskets.

"Happy packed us a wonderful lunch," Roxanne explained. "There's food enough for everyone."

Sabrina clapped her hands together.

"This is wonderful news! Zazz!" she called to the butterfly. "Hurry and tell everyone that our picnic celebration is about to begin. I have something I must do."

Zazz flew to the Gilliwags, who were napping in the reeds. Then she zoomed to the Nymphs, who were frolicking in the pool at the base of Bluebonnet Falls. Then she hurried to find the Striders. They were skating near the shore of Blue Lake.

Gurt the Gilliwag spread a tablecloth on the grass and set out the royal china. Demetra, Emily, and Roxanne unpacked the picnic baskets.

While everyone prepared for their feast, Sabrina looked for Oona.

She found her in the murky waters near the Willow-that-Weeps. Oona clutched the golden basket in her mouth.

"What are you doing?" Sabrina gasped.

"Don't you remember? That basket is poisoned!"

Oona set the basket on a floating log. "I'm going to take this basket with its poisoned food to the bottom of our lake."

Sabrina's eyes widened. "Below the Deep Dark?"

Oona nodded. "I'm taking it to a place so deep that no creature will ever find it."

"But won't you join our picnic first?" Sabrina asked. "Roxanne brought an entire feast."

Oona smiled sadly. "I would love to join your feast. And maybe one day I will. But for now, I must do this. I want to make sure that Lord Bleak doesn't harm one more creature in our beautiful lake."

Sabrina stepped onto the floating log near the lake creature. She wrapped her arms around Oona's neck. "You have done much to help us. Is there any way we can repay your kindness?"

Oona closed her eyes in thought. When she opened them again she said, "I have been so lonely for so long. The best gift you could give me is your friendship."

"That you have," Sabrina promised. "And will always have."

With that, Oona scooped up the poisoned basket and plunged into the lake.

Sabrina stared at the ripple of water where Oona had just been.

And for one moment, Sabrina was certain she saw a beautiful mermaid with sea-green eyes and skin the color of pearls.

About the Authors

JAHNNA N. MALCOLM stands for Jahnna "and" Malcolm. Jahnna Beecham and Malcolm Hillgartner are married and write together. They have written over seventy books for kids. Jahnna N. Malcolm have written about ballerinas, horses, ghosts, singing cowgirls, and green slime.

Before Jahnna and Malcolm wrote books, they were actors. They met on the stage where Malcolm was playing a prince. And they were married on the stage where Jahnna was playing a princess.

Now they have their own little prince and princess: Dash and Skye. They all live in Ashland, Oregon, with their big red dog, Ruby, and their fluffy little white dog, Clarence.

A World of Dazzling Magic...

THE JEWEL KINGDOM

One of the Princesses is missing!

Roxanne isn't ready to become the Ruby Princess — she would rather climb trees and ride dragons. She runs away...and a *fake* ruby princess takes her place! What will become of the Jewel Kingdom?

A beautiful ruby-red necklace with this book!

THE JEWEL KINGDOM #1
The Ruby Princess Runs Away

Jahnna N. Malcolm

LITTLE 🍎 APPLE®

Here are some of our favorite Little Apples.

There are fun times ahead with kids just like you in Little Apple books! Once you take a bite out of a Little Apple—you'll want to read more!

Reading Excitement for Kids with BIG Appetites!

☐ NA45899-X **Amber Brown Is Not a Crayon**
Paula Danziger $2.99

☐ NA93425-2 **Amber Brown Goes Fourth**
Paula Danziger $2.99

☐ NA50207-7 **You Can't Eat Your Chicken Pox, Amber Brown**
Paula Danziger $2.99

☐ NA42833-0 **Catwings** Ursula K. LeGuin $2.95

☐ NA42832-2 **Catwings Return** Ursula K. LeGuin $3.50

☐ NA41821-1 **Class Clown** Johanna Hurwitz $2.99

☐ NA42400-9 **Five True Horse Stories**
Margaret Davidson $2.99

☐ NA43868-9 **The Haunting of Grade Three**
Grace Maccarone $2.99

☐ NA40966-2 **Rent a Third Grader** B.B. Hiller $2.99

☐ NA41944-7 **The Return of the Third Grade Ghost Hunters**
Grace Maccarone $2.99

☐ NA42031-3 **Teacher's Pet** Johanna Hurwitz $3.50

Available wherever you buy books...or use the coupon below.

SCHOLASTIC INC., P.O. Box 7502, 2931 East McCarty Street, Jefferson City, MO 65102

Please send me the books I have checked above. I am enclosing $ _____ (please add $2.00 to cover shipping and handling). Send check or money order—no cash or C.O.D.s please.

Name_____

Address_____

City_____State/Zip_____

Please allow four to six weeks for delivery. Offer good in the U.S.A. only. Sorry, mail orders are not available to residents of Canada. Prices subject to change.

LA996